This book of
Sandshoes at the Beach

Belongs to:

_____

Sandshoes at the Beach

ISBN: 978-1-60920-026-8
Printed in the United States of America
©2011 by Catherine Eddy & Joann Krupnek

Illustrations by Joann Krupnek
Cover and interior design by Ajoyin Publishing, Inc.

Library of Congress Cataloging-in-Publication Data

API
Ajoyin Publishing, Inc.
P.O. 342
Three Rivers, MI 49093
www.ajoyin.com

Please direct your inquiries to admin@ajoyin.com

A Max & Maggie Story

Sandshoes
at the beach

Written by Catherine J. Eddy
Illustrated by Joann J. Krupnek

Notice how much fun Whiskers the cat will have as she goes to the beach in a basket. She is a most unusual cat because most cats do not like the water or the beach!

Cathy and Joann are sisters on a new adventure in life. A dream come true for both!

Cathy and Joann both dedicate this book to their husbands for their continued support of their new adventure in life. To Cathy's husband, Walt Eddy, and Joann's husband, Jerry Krupnek.

To our two red-headed inspirations, Elizabeth and Katelyn Fisher, our nieces.

Also, a dedication to the pelicans, seagulls and sanderlings. These birds provide many hours of delightful entertainment when we go out bird watching. We enjoy this activity on the many miles of public sand beaches everywhere.

৵

Come and Count with Whiskers

Look for Whiskers the cat as you read "Sandbox Sandshoes go to the Beach." Whiskers will appear somewhere on each page in the story.

Each time you read the story, the following suggestions will help you make up your own rules or you may use any combination of rules for counting Whiskers:

- If you only see Whiskers' tail, will you count it?
- If you only see Whiskers' head, will you count it?
- If you only see Whiskers' whiskers, will they count?
- Or will only the whole body of Whiskers' count?

Now get ready to count and have fun looking for Whiskers.

"Maggie, it is your turn to introduce us in our new book," said Max.

"Thank you, Max." I am Maggie and Max is my twin brother. We both have red hair, freckles, and green eyes. We have a fluffy yellow cat, with green eyes, named Whiskers. We love to play in the sand and enjoy our favorite game of "Sandbox Sandshoes." Today, we will play our sandshoes game at the beach. We do not need a sand pail or shovel, just our hands and feet. Our imagination will be our guide."

"Mom and Dad put sunscreen on us so we do not get a sun-burn from the hot sun today. Sunburns can hurt," cautioned Max.

Maggie laughed and replied, "Whiskers will not need sun-screen. She has a fur coat to protect her skin."

The twins giggled at their cat in her fur coat. "Max, I am ready to play our 'Sandbox Sandshoes' game and the beach will make a very big sandbox for us to play in," suggested Maggie.

"Hand in hand
We will pile the sand
Upon our feet
And sandshoes we will make,
Oh, the adventures we shall take."

As Maggie makes a pair of sandshoes, she sings, "What will I be? Where will I go? What will I see? Let my imagination be my guide. I know! I will be a lovely mermaid sitting, upon a rock, by the ocean. I will make mermaid fins, of sand, for my feet. Each day I will sit upon my rock and watch the fish as they swim by. Because I just know that is what a mermaid would do."

Imagination is fun, and imagination can be funny!

Now Max takes a turn and sings, "What will I be? Where will I go? What will I see? Let my imagination be my guide. I know! I will make swim fins, of sand, for my feet. Then as I swim in my fins, I will see seashells, starfish and all the fish that live in the ocean. I may even see a turtle too!"

Imagination is fun, and imagination can be funny!

"Maggie, I am going to make tennis shoes of sand and go running on the beach. I will be a great runner and there will be miles and miles of sand for me to run on."

"Max! That is a great idea. I will run with you too. Our sandbox is fun to run in, but there is more room for us to run together on the beach," answered Maggie.

They both laughed and sang as they ran for miles and miles on the beach.

"Sandshoes are for dreaming;
Sandshoes are for fun.
Wear them in the sand and sun;
Sandshoes are fun for everyone!"

"Max! I am tired of running for miles and miles on the beach. My feet are hot and tired. I need to stop running and rest my feet," exclaimed Maggie. "I agree Maggie. My feet are hot and tired too!" replied Max. The twins sigh with pleasure as they stick their feet into the cool, wet sand and sing:

"Dig in, dig in feet
The sand is cool and wet.
Dig in, dig in deep feet
And feel how nice
On hot tired feet."

Now with their feet in the sand, the twins sing out:

"What will we be?

Where will we go?

What will we see?

Let your imaginations be your guide."

"Max, we can make sandshoes to go bird watching in," suggested Maggie.

"I would love to go bird watching with you Maggie. We will be called bird watchers," replied Max.

Maggie burst out laughing, "Look Max! There is a seagull sitting on the head of a pelican. You will not see a seagull sitting on top of a pelican every day. It may be hard to believe, but the pelican and the seagull will sometimes go fishing together."

Max chuckled and said, "I think they would like to have fish for their lunch today."

The twins laughed at the silliness of the pelican and the seagull waiting for the fish to swim by.

"Look Max! It looks like the pelican found fish and is ready to go fishing. The pelican and seagull will dive together for fish. The seagull will get to eat leftover fish that the pelican does not eat," explained Maggie.

"There will be fish for lunch for the pelican and the seagull. I think I would like my fish cooked please," requested Max.

The children laughed as they watched the pelican and the seagull go fishing together.
Hmmmm. What do you suppose Whiskers is thinking about?

Eat fish, fish, fish
Morning, noon and night–
Breakfast, lunch and dinner
They sure are a winner,
Eat fish, fish, fish.

Imagination is fun, and imagination can be funny!

"Oh, Maggie, look at the sanderlings playing with the waves. It looks like a game of tag when the sanderlings chase after the waves," exclaimed Max.

Maggie laughed and said, "The sanderlings only look like they are chasing waves. They are looking for waterbugs to eat. The sanderlings are working very hard for their lunch. I am glad we do not have to work as hard as sanderlings for our lunch."

"Or eat waterbugs," chuckled Max.

"Run sanderlings, Run! Here come the waves to chase you back to shore. And tag, it will be your turn to chase the waves back out again. Do you think the sanderlings' legs get tired from running in and out of the waves just to eat their lunch?" asked Maggie.

Max laughed and answered, "I would call it exercising while you eat."

Chasing the waves look like fun, so the twins jump out of their sandshoes and run out to chase the waves. Max and Maggie shout with joy at the waves.

"Run waves run, here we come
We will chase you, we will catch you–
And with our feet, we will splash you.
Tag waves! You are it!
Now chase us, catch us, splash us–
And we will play the game again!"

"Run! Here come the waves to chase us back," shout the twins in excited voices.

Waves splashing—

Children laughing—

As they play,

On a warm summer day.

HANG ON WHISKERS. HANG ON TIGHT!

Max and Maggie are very tired and ready to end their day of fun. Max yawned and sleepily suggests, "I am tired and ready to go home. I would like to write in my book about all the fun I had today. I call my book my daily journal."

Maggie yawned and sleepily answered back, "Max, I also keep a journal and in my journal I also draw pictures. Each day I try to write or draw a picture about my day. Yes, when we journal we will always remember the fun we had today."

Shhhhhhh! Sandshoes are sleeping. They had too much fun today! Whiskers, did you have too much fun today? Shhhhhhhh! Whiskers is sleeping too!

"Sandshoes are for dreaming;
Sandshoes are for fun.
Wear them in the sand and sun;
Sandshoes are fun for everyone!"

www.ingramcontent.com/pod-product-compliance
Lightning Source LLC
Chambersburg PA
CBHW041001170626
46815CB00002B/108